RED FOX

A Red Fox Book
Published by Random House Children's Books
20 Vauxhall Bridge Road, London SW1V 2SA
A division of Random House UK Ltd
London Melbourne Sydney Auckland
Johannesburg and agencies throughout the world
Copyright © 1984 Marc Brown
3 5 7 9 10 8 6 4 2
First published in the United States of America by
Little, Brown & Company and simultaneously in Canada by
Little, Brown & Company (Canada) Ltd 1984
First published in Great Britain by Red Fox 1997
All rights reserved
Printed in Hong Kong
RANDOM HOUSE UK Limited Reg. No. 954009
ISBN 0 09 921922 0

For my Grandma Thora,
who taught me about giving

Arthur and D.W. had been present-hunting
for a long time.
"For heaven's sake," D.W. said. "This shop
is full of presents. Pick one and let's go!"

"It has to be just right," said Arthur. "I want Santa to like it."

"Well, hurry up," said D.W. "I want to get home and see if Grandma's there and how many presents she's brought me."

At home, D.W. added ten more things she wanted
to her Christmas list and went over it in red pencil.
Arthur and D.W. cheered when they heard the car
in the driveway.
"Grandma, are there any presents in there for me?"
asked D.W.

"Grandma, do you think Santa would like new mittens or gloves?" asked Arthur.
"Whatever happened to, 'Hello, I'm glad to see you'?" asked Grandma Thora.

After dinner, everyone relaxed.

"Look," said D.W. "I teached Killer a trick."

"Taught," said Grandma. "You taught Killer a trick."

But D.W. wasn't listening. She had seen something on television to add to her list.

"Arthur, what's the matter?" asked Grandma.

"I haven't found the right gift for Santa," said Arthur.

"Only two shopping days left," D.W. reminded him.

The next day, Arthur, D.W., and their friends went shopping. Killer went too.
Arthur searched the entire shop and still couldn't find the perfect gift for Santa.
"What's the big problem?" asked D.W. "I can see a hundred things I want. Let's go and tell Santa."

"Santa, what would *you* like for Christmas?" asked Arthur.
"Ho, ho, ho," laughed Santa. "You just leave the giving to me."
D.W. had her picture taken patting Santa's tummy.

Buster was next.

"Santa, be careful coming down the chimney at our house. My parents always forget to put the fire out."

"Ho, ho, ho," said Santa. "Don't worry. I'll use the front door."

Then it was Francine's turn.

"Have you been a good little girl?" asked Santa.

"Oh, yes," smiled Francine. "I'm always good."

"Always?" asked Santa.

Afterwards, Buster treated them all to ice cream.

Arthur could hardly finish his root beer float.

He had only one more shopping day left.

"Look!" said Francine. "Santa eats ice cream!"

"I'll have a banana split with six scoops of bubble-gum ice cream," said Santa.

"With hot fudge, whipped cream, and nut topping."

"I'll say he eats ice cream," said D.W.

At home, Arthur asked his family for help.
"How about a nice colourful tie?" said Father.

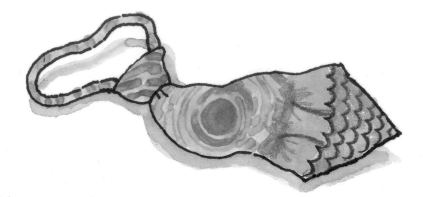

"Aftershave is always a good gift," said Mother.

"I bet Santa could do with some toasty-warm
long johns," said Grandma.

"Arthur, you're taking this shopping too seriously," said D.W. "Just do what I do. Get everyone the same thing."

That afternoon, everyone was getting ready
to go carol-singing.
But Arthur didn't have time for Christmas carols.
Time was running out.
"Please come too," begged D.W. "I'll be the
only kid. And besides, Mrs Tibble always
gives us a present and hot chocolate."

Arthur went window shopping instead, hoping that
it would give him an idea for Santa's present.
Santa was ho-ho-ho-ing and drinking a diet
root beer at the petrol station.

Moments later Santa was at the Golden Chopstick,
eating subgum chow goo.

Then Santa must have run to the burger bar on the corner
of North and Main Street.
The waitress shouted Santa's order to the cook.
"One double cheeseburger with special relish and
extra large fries!"
"Santa sure eats a lot," thought Arthur.

Finally Arthur went home.
He hadn't seen a single thing in any of the
shop windows that Santa might like.
Santa was on TV eating Papa Piper's
pickled peppers.
"That's it!" said Arthur.
He started making his list.

Arthur counted his money.
"D.W.," he said in his sweetest voice.
"OK, how much do you need?" asked D.W.
"But only if you promise to stop being
such a grouch."

The next morning, Arthur gave D.W. half of his
list. He took the other half.

D.W. had to keep Killer out of the kitchen
while Arthur made Santa's present.
"What's all that noise?" asked Father.
"Arthur is making a mess," reported D.W.
The kitchen door opened, and Arthur sneezed.
"Mom, how many cups of pepper in pickled
peppers?" he asked.
"Maybe I should help," said Mother.
"No, please," said Arthur. "I want to make
Santa's present myself. Just tell me
how many sticks of gum in subgum chow goo?"
"Poor Santa," said D.W.

Hours later, Arthur whistled while
he laid the table for Santa.
"What's *that*?" asked Father.
"Pickled peppers, a hot fudge sundae with
bubble-gum ice cream, and subgum chow goo.
I sort of combined all of Santa's favourite
food," Arthur explained.

"What's that big lumpy thing that's moving?"
asked Grandma.
"A pizza to go," said Arthur. "With
everything."
"If you want Santa to come, you'd better
go to bed," said Mother.
"If we want Santa to come," thought D.W.,
"we'd better do something about that food."

D.W. couldn't fall asleep.

"I have to do something," she thought. "Poor Arthur worked so hard. But if Santa gets one whiff of Arthur's present, he'll never set foot in the dining room – let alone eat any of it." Careful to avoid the squeaky step, D.W. tiptoed downstairs in the dark.

The next morning,
Arthur was the first one up.
"Santa ate it all!" he cried.
"And he left a note!"

Dear Arthur,
You were so nice to take
the time to find out my
favorite foods and make
them.
Thank you.
You also teached me about
the Christmas spirit.
Love,
SANtA
P.S.
Aren't you lucky to have such
a nice little sister?